Get to know the girls of

BY
THALIA KALKIPSAKIS

ILLUSTRATIONS BY
ASH OSWALD

FEIWEL AND FRIENDS
New York

A FEIWEL AND FRIENDS BOOK
An Imprint of Macmillan

THE WORST GYMNAST. Text copyright © 2005 by
Thalia Kalkipsakis. Illustration and design copyright
© 2005 by Hardie Grant Egmont. All rights reserved.
Printed June 2010 in the United States of America
by R. R. Donnelley & Sons Company, Harrisonburg,
Virginia. For information, address Feiwel and Friends,
175 Fifth Avenue, New York, NY 10010.

Library of Congress Cataloging-in-Publication Data
Available

ISBN: 978-0-312-34642-3

First published in Australia by E2, an imprint of Hardie
Grant Egmont. Illustration and design by Ash Oswald.

First published in the United States by Feiwel and
Friends, an imprint of Macmillan.

Feiwel and Friends logo designed by Filomena Tuosto

First U.S. Edition: 2007

10 9 8 7 6 5 4

www.feiwelandfriends.com

CHAPTER *ONE

Gemma stood at the start of the runway, ready to run. She pictured a handspring in her mind—*legs together, butt tucked in . . . up and over the vault.* But she didn't run yet. She was waiting for Michael to nod his head.

Michael was Gemma's gymnastics coach. He kicked a safety mat into place, then stood next to the vault, ready to help Gemma over.

Finally, Michael nodded his head.

Gemma wiped her hands on her legs and looked at the vault. Then she ran.

She ran fast, pumping her arms.

As Gemma ran up to the vault, Michael reached in to help her over.

But as Gemma jumped, her foot slipped. Her legs flew apart and her butt stuck out. She did it all wrong. She was just about to crash into the vault when Michael pushed her up and over—*legs apart, butt out, almost over . . .*

Thud!

One of Gemma's legs—out of control —hit Michael in the face. Gemma landed on her back, with her arms and legs out.

It had been a very bad vault.

Gemma lay on her back, surprised that she had made it over. That had been close. Was anything hurt? Nothing.

Then Gemma remembered the thud. She rolled off the mat.

Michael stood in the same spot with his face in his hands.

"Sorry," Gemma said quietly.

This was bad. Was Michael alright?

"I'm so sorry," Gemma said a bit louder.

Michael lifted his head.

Blood trickled from his nose onto the palm of his hand.

"Are you alright?" Gemma asked, but it felt like a silly question. His nose was bleeding.

Michael looked at Gemma and shook his head. He wiped his nose with a tissue. "Team meeting," he said, and walked away.

The rest of the team was sitting at the start of the runway. The four girls sat in a row with their mouths dropped open and their eyes wide. They looked as if they had just seen a ghost. Either that, or the worst vault ever.

Gemma sat down next to her best friend, Kathy. Kathy had dark curly hair that bounced when she moved, and a broad smile. Gemma thought Kathy was beautiful.

Kathy looked at Gemma as if to say, *We're in for it now*.

Gemma raised her eyebrows back at Kathy. Was she about to be kicked off the team?

Michael was a good coach, the best at the club. But he yelled a lot. Most of the gymnasts were afraid of him. He had hairy eyebrows that made it look like he was always frowning.

"You don't have to like me. But you have to listen to me!" Michael would often yell at the girls.

So kicking him in the face was not very good at all.

"OK, level six," Michael wiped his nose again. "It's time to talk."

The five girls sat in a row. For the next ten minutes, they listened to Michael. He talked, he frowned, he yelled. For the whole ten minutes, the girls didn't move.

Gemma loved gymnastics. Her school friends called her "Gemma the gymnast." But they had no idea how hard Gemma worked at it.

She had worked so hard that she was

now on a real team. Being on a team meant that she had her own routines and entered competitions. Soon, the level six team would go to the state finals.

But being on a team meant more than that. It meant that Michael was Gemma's coach. And Michael was the top coach. Some of the girls on his teams had even made it to the Olympics. So Gemma was delighted to be on Michael's team.

Now Michael talked about working hard—harder than ever before. He talked about what it takes to be the best.

"It's time to get serious," he said.

At the end of his talk, Michael sent the rest of the team to the bars.

Then he looked at Gemma. "Let's go to my office," he said.

Gemma looked at the floor and nodded. She swallowed a big lump in her throat. This was it. Her life as a gymnast was over.

She was about to be kicked off the team.

CHAPTER *TWO*

Gemma sat in Michael's office, looking at her feet. She had already said she was sorry for kicking Michael in the face. Now she didn't know what to say. Inside, she felt terrible.

Michael was writing and frowning. He wiped his nose with a tissue, which was now bloodred.

Michael put down his pen and handed Gemma a sheet of paper.

"Here is some extra strength work for you," Michael said.

Gemma looked at the paper.

"When the other girls start stretching, you do this," Michael said, and sniffed.

"OK," Gemma said. Extra strength work? Did that mean she wasn't being kicked off the team?

"Now go to the bars, Gemma," Michael said, without smiling.

"OK." Gemma smiled to herself.

She wasn't being kicked off the team! This was great.

When Gemma came down to the bars, the rest of the team crowded around her.

"What did Michael say?" Naomi asked.

Her eyes were wide with worry through the smudge of chalk dust on her face.

Naomi was the best on the team. She was small and strong. Naomi, Anika, and Fiona had all been on the level six team last year, and Michael had kept them down. But all the girls thought Naomi should have gone up to level seven.

"I have to do extra strength training," Gemma said. "That's not too bad, is it?"

"Not too bad," Kathy smiled.

The other girls nodded.

All through the bars, Gemma started feeling better. She was still on the team. Plus, she was good on bars. She loved the swinging, rolling feeling as she swung between the bars—*swing up, hip circle around, pike over the lower bar to catch the high bar*. It was almost like flying.

But when it was time to do the extra strength training, Gemma started feeling bad again. The extra strength was hard work. And there was lots of it.

Gemma did so many chin-ups, her arms felt like they were on fire. Then she had to hold a handstand, followed by running and jumping while holding weights. Last of all, she had to do push-ups. Soon her arms and legs started to hurt.

Gemma looked over at the rest of the team. They were stretching their legs and talking. They looked happy. Kathy looked

over at Gemma with a broad smile. Gemma
smiled back, but inside she felt sad.

Gemma liked stretching. She could
do the splits on both sides already. It felt
good to stretch her legs after the energy of
gymnastics.

But now, Gemma had to do extra work

on her own. Her whole body hurt.

When Gemma's dad came to pick her up at the end of the class, Gemma felt too tired to move. She slumped in the car seat like a rag doll. She was almost too tired to put her seatbelt on.

"How's my gym bunny?" Gemma's dad asked.

"OK," Gemma said quietly. What should she say? *I kicked my coach in the face. It was the worst class ever.*

"Are you OK, Gem?" her dad asked.

"Yup," Gemma said. She didn't know what else to say. She was too tired to talk.

Gemma looked out the car window at the bright lights zooming past.

Now it all started to make sense.

Gemma had kicked Michael, but he wasn't going to kick Gemma off the team. He was going to make her pay in other ways. He had given her all that extra work to make Gemma pay for kicking him.

Gemma turned her head to the side, so her dad couldn't see a tear spilling down her cheek.

She still felt bad for kicking Michael. But it had been an accident. She had said she was sorry. What if you do something wrong, but saying you're sorry isn't good enough? How do you fix things then?

Gemma loved gymnastics. She lived for gymnastics. But now it had all turned bad.

CHAPTER THREE

Two days later, it was time for the next gymnastics class. Gemma's shoulder muscles still felt sore from the extra strength work, and her legs still felt tired. She didn't feel ready for another training session, let alone extra strength all over again.

While the team warmed up, Gemma scrunched up her face in pain. It hurt simply to lift her arms in the air.

"Sore muscles, huh?" Kathy said.

"That strength work was really bad," Gemma said, swinging her arms stiffly.

"Yeah, we could see," Anika said. She tilted her head in sympathy.

"Do you have to do it again today?" Fiona asked.

"Yeah," Gemma said sadly. But it felt good talking about it. She hadn't said anything at home or at school about the extra strength. At least the girls on the team knew what it was like. Even if they didn't have to do extra strength training, they knew how Gemma was feeling.

"You'll be alright, Gem," Kathy said, and

tickled Gemma under the arm. "You can do it." Gemma giggled and jumped back. Somehow, her sore arms didn't matter so much when she was with the team.

"Glad it's not me!" Naomi said, and she leaned back into a walkover.

Then Michael walked up, and the talking stopped.

"OK, level six," Michael said. "Floor and beam today." He put his hands on his hips. "Start warming up the dance leaps from your floor routines, please."

Michael walked to the edge of the floor and folded his arms in front of him. His eyebrows seemed to be stuck in a frown.

Quickly, the girls lined up at the corner of the floor and started leaping across it.

Gemma liked the floor routines, especially the dance part. She could leap high and split her legs wide. It felt like she had an extra lift as she split her legs in the air.

Gemma spread her arms like a real dancer and practiced her favorite leap sequence—*run, run, split leap, run, run, side leap, turn . . . run, switch leap*. Quickly, she swapped her legs in the air. She felt light and graceful.

"Good, Gemma." Michael stopped frowning for a moment.

Gemma smiled to herself. Michael didn't praise her very often.

"Start working on your tumbles now, Gemma," Michael said.

"Tumbles already?" Gemma frowned. She had only done one leap sequence. Now she had to start on the acrobatic part of her routine.

"Do as I say, Gemma." Michael suddenly looked cross. "You have a lot of work to do before the state finals."

Gemma nodded and ran to the other side of the floor. She started some backflips and somersaults to warm up. Was this because she had kicked Michael?

Tumbling by herself was no fun. Secretly, Gemma felt almost scared each time she tumbled. She always felt a little bit out of control, as though landing on her feet needed some luck.

"Don't think I'm not watching you," Michael yelled to the rest of the team. "OK, Gemma, let's see the tumbles from your floor routine."

Gemma breathed out hard. She wiped her hands on her legs, and ran—*run, run, round-off, backflip, back tuck, land.*

That wasn't too bad.

"Do it again, Gemma," Michael said. "I want to see that faster and higher."

Gemma sighed and glanced at Kathy, who shrugged her shoulders.

"Naomi, keep working on those leaps!" Michael yelled.

Gemma sighed again and ran harder for her next tumbling pass. She managed to jump just a bit higher into the back tuck.

"OK," Michael said. "Again."

Gemma kept tumbling until her arms ached. She felt lonely and tired.

Finally, the other girls were called to tumble, too. At least Gemma wasn't alone. She could feel the girls lining up behind her, even though they couldn't talk.

When it was Naomi's turn, she did a near-perfect tumble right away.

"Good, Naomi," Michael almost smiled. "Very good layout."

Naomi smiled as she walked back to the line. "Then why didn't you let me do level seven?" Naomi said quietly, so Michael couldn't hear.

The rest of gym class went quickly until —all too soon—it was time for Gemma to do the extra strength work.

As the rest of the team went over to stretch, Kathy whispered, "Go, Gem!"

Gemma tried to smile, but she really wanted to cry. Her arms were so tired from the extra tumbling that she didn't know how she would get through the extra strength training. It didn't seem possible.

Slowly Gemma started the chin-ups. She pulled up and her chin just cleared the bar.

"One," came Michael's voice from the other end of the gym. "I'm watching you, Gemma."

Gemma's eyes narrowed. She pulled up to the bar again, faster this time because she was angry.

"Two," came Michael's voice.

Gemma didn't know what it felt like to hate someone, but she thought she was starting to hate Michael.

Gemma stayed angry through the chin-ups and finished them OK. Even though her legs were tired, she still found energy for the running and jumping. But when it came time for the push-ups, Gemma's arms stopped working.

Each time she tried to push up, her arms shook and wouldn't hold her up.

"Just get those push-ups done and you're finished," Michael said as he stood over Gemma.

Gemma tried once more, but her arms

just wouldn't move. She lay on her stomach, her arms shaking. She wanted to scream.

"Had enough?" Michael asked.

Gemma nodded. It didn't matter what Michael said now, she just couldn't do it.

"OK, quick stretch, then go home." Michael's voice almost sounded kind.

Gemma stood up slowly, but she couldn't look at Michael. If she did, she would want to yell at him. *This isn't fair! I didn't kick you on purpose.* She would either yell or she would burst into tears.

But Gemma stayed quiet through stretching and even in the locker room. As she walked out the gym door that night, she wished she was never coming back.

It was no fun at all, being the worst gymnast.

CHAPTER FOUR

The next class was usually Gemma's favorite—first normal gymastics, then dance in the studio. But Gemma didn't want to go. She didn't want to see Michael ever again.

As she packed her gym bag at home after school, Gemma thought about pretending to be sick. She walked slowly to the front door.

"Mom, maybe I'll stay home today," Gemma said. "I think I'm sick."

Maybe I'll stay home today.

"Sick?" Gemma's mom felt Gemma's forehead. "Sick where?"

Gemma was quiet. She wanted to tell her mom about the extra strength work. But that would also mean telling her about kicking Michael. And Gemma didn't want to do that. She didn't want to tell her mom she was the worst on the team.

"My shoulders are sore," Gemma said finally.

"Sore muscles?" her mom smiled. "We can fix that."

Gemma's mom walked away and came back with some heat rub. "All the top athletes swear by this stuff," she said.

Slowly, her mom rubbed the cream on Gemma's shoulders.

"You know, Gemma . . . " said her mom. "You're doing some pretty tricky gymnastics these days."

Gemma stayed quiet.

"You're doing the real sport. The hard stuff. Someone on your team might even go all the way."

Gemma thought of Naomi, but she said nothing.

"So it's going to hurt sometimes, sweetheart," said Gemma's mom. She wiped her hands on a tissue. "But promise me one thing."

Gemma looked at her mom. Her shoulders felt warm and didn't hurt so much now.

"If it ever feels like you're going to really hurt yourself," said Gemma's mom, "if it ever feels like it hurts *too* much, then you stop. Don't let Michael push you too hard."

Just slightly, Gemma nodded. Was Michael pushing her too hard already?

"Sometimes that man takes things too far," her mom said, opening the front door.

Slowly and quietly, Gemma followed her mom to the car.

In the locker room before gymnastics, Naomi held her nose. "Ick! Who stinks?" she said.

Anika stood up and looked at Gemma, but Gemma stayed quiet. She kind of liked the strong smell of the heat rub.

"Dance today, Gemma," said Anika. "That should cheer you up."

Gemma nodded. She liked Anika.

"Yuck, dance," said Naomi. "Who needs it?" Even though Naomi was the best on the team, she wasn't the best at dance. She looked out of place in the dance studio.

All through training, Gemma tried her

hardest. Even though she was tired, she didn't want Michael to yell at her. In fact, she didn't even want him to talk to her. She jumped high, she ran hard. She did her very best. She made sure Michael had nothing to talk to her about.

Sometimes, Gemma could feel Michael watching her. He stood with his arms crossed, watching.

At those times, Gemma tried even harder. But Michael said nothing. He let Gemma dance without doing the extra strength work.

In some ways, it was the best gymnastics class in a long time.

CHAPTER FIVE

Over the weekend, Gemma still felt sore and tired. She lay on the couch watching TV until her mom turned it off. Then Gemma lay on the couch watching nothing.

Her body felt exhausted. But more than that, her mind felt exhausted, too. She was tired of feeling sorry for kicking Michael. She was tired of trying hard. She was tired of everything.

Slowly, Gemma dozed off, and woke up to see her mom standing over her, holding a sandwich.

"Hungry?" asked Gemma's mom.

Gemma sat up. As she started eating, she realized that she was very hungry. Peanut butter and jelly on fresh white bread tasted great.

After a while, her mom scratched her chin. "Hey, why don't you put on your favorite video? You know, that Olympics one?" She winked. "I can tell you've been working hard at gymnastics."

"Great idea. Thanks, Mom." Gemma jumped up to find the video. Suddenly, she didn't feel quite so tired.

The video showed the world's top gymnasts competing in the individual finals. Gemma had watched it so many times, she felt like she knew all of the routines by heart.

But today the routines looked different. Where she used to just watch with her mouth open in wonder, now she understood what was happening. Gemma could already do some of the simple moves herself. She could even tell where the gymnasts lost marks.

Gemma smiled. She had learned so much since starting level six.

Then, as she watched one of her favorite gymnasts on the beam, Gemma noticed something.

She stopped the video and rewound it.

There it was again—a switch leap. Just like the one Gemma did in her own floor routine, except on the beam.

That started Gemma thinking.

She already had a split leap in her beam routine. Could she do a switch leap instead? Could she leap high enough to land safely on the beam?

Gemma stood up and marked out a line on the living-room floor. She tried the leap—*run, run, switch* . . .

No.

Gemma landed in a crumpled heap. She hardly had enough time to split her legs, let alone swap them for a second

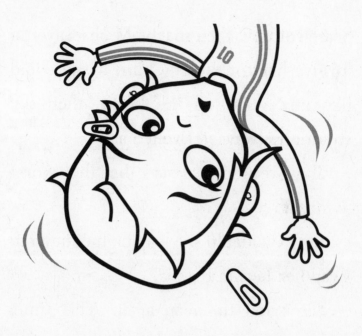

split. To do a switch leap on the beam, she would have to jump much higher than that.

Gemma rewound the video again. She watched closer than ever before.

Her mind buzzed with the new idea.

If Gemma could do a really good

beam routine, then maybe Michael would forgive her for kicking him. If she could be extra good on the beam, then she wouldn't always get yelled at.

She wouldn't always be the worst gymnast.

But how could she leap high enough to swap her legs in the air?

She tried the leap again. This time, Gemma tried to leap extra high.

As she ran into the leap, her arm flew to the side and hit the TV cabinet.

Thwack!

Gemma rubbed her arm. Ouch.

"Everything OK?" Gemma's mom asked from the kitchen.

"Just trying a few things out," said Gemma.

Her mom walked into the room and picked up a glass vase. "Just like the good old days," she said as she walked out of the room with the vase.

CHAPTER SIX

Over the following weeks, Gemma started looking forward to gymnastics again. Her muscles didn't feel quite so sore and the extra strength work didn't feel quite so hard.

These days, Gemma was much stronger, too. She could feel it when she picked up her school bag full of books. She could feel it as she bounded up the stairs. She could feel it when she turned on a faucet after her dad had turned it off hard.

Plus, Gemma felt stronger at gymnastics. Jumping high into a back tuck was still hard, but it didn't make Gemma so tired anymore. Now when she did a handspring, she would push off the vault and feel her body lift in response.

Gemma's body was doing what she wanted it to do.

It was such a good feeling.

Gemma didn't tell anyone about her new plan for the beam. But she practiced the new leap at home. She was getting better at the switch leap, but she could barely land on the line.

She kept practicing, but the state finals

were getting closer. Gemma was almost out of time.

One day on the floor, Gemma decided to practice her new leap instead of normal leaps.

Gemma scanned the floor. Michael was talking to Fiona and moving his arms as though they were legs doing a leap. The other girls were leaping across the floor.

Quickly, Gemma found a crease on the other side of the floor, with the rest of the team between her and Michael.

She started working on the switch leap, over and over.

Run, run, switch leap, land . . . wobble.

Again.

She could leap OK, but she still couldn't stop that wobble.

After a few leaps, Gemma scratched her head. She had to leap higher so she had more time to balance at the end. But how?

Then Gemma noticed Kathy watching her. Kathy had a strange look on her face.

She didn't understand what Gemma was doing.

Gemma started walking towards Kathy. It was time to tell Kathy about the new leap. They were best friends, after all.

But as Gemma walked over to Kathy, Michael called the team to start on tumbles— everyone, that was, except Gemma.

"Those were the worst leaps you've ever done, Gemma." Michael shook his head, frowning.

Gemma gulped. He had seen her!

"They weren't even part of your routine!" Michael growled.

Not my floor routine, thought Gemma, but she stayed quiet. She couldn't tell Michael about the new leap. Not yet. Not before she could land it on the beam.

"Keep working on your leaps, Gemma," Michael said. "Properly, this time."

As she worked on her leaps alone, Gemma grumbled to herself. She had worked so hard, and he still yelled at her.

It doesn't matter how hard I work!

But when it was time for the extra strength work, Michael came over.

"Skip the extra strength work today, Gemma," he said. "You're doing well with your routines." Then he mumbled, "Except for those leaps . . . "

Gemma looked up. Did Michael just say something nice to her? Even when he said she was doing well, he did it with a growl.

Gemma bounded over to the rest of the team to stretch, and Michael left the girls on their own. They moved to a corner of the floor and slid into splits.

"So how does it feel to be back with the team?" Naomi asked. She leaned over to the side so that she didn't stretch much at all.

"Pretty good," Gemma said. She pushed down a bit harder.

Now that her legs were stronger, they felt a bit tight.

"Well, this is how it should be," Anika said. "Michael shouldn't split us up."

As they moved through all the different stretches, the girls talked about their routines and the state finals. Fiona was nervous about the competition. Kathy couldn't wait. They all thought Naomi had a chance to win the trophy.

As they talked and whispered, Gemma felt glad to be stretching with the team again. She felt as though she knew these girls better than her friends at school.

They all knew what it was like to live for gymnastics.

CHAPTER

SEVEN

In the locker room after class, Gemma whispered to Kathy, "Come down to the beams with me."

"Why?" Kathy asked, doing up her shoelace.

"I want to show you something," Gemma said.

When the other girls had gone, Gemma and Kathy sneaked down to the beam area. The level sevens were warming up by themselves. Michael was nowhere to be seen.

Gemma dropped her bag by the low beam and slipped off her shoes.

"I'm going to add a new leap to my beam routine," Gemma said.

"Is that what you were doing on floor today?" Kathy asked.

"Yup," Gemma nodded. "What do you think of this?"

She stood next to the low beam and did a switch leap on the floor. She just managed to swap her legs in the air before landing. Then she jumped up onto the low beam, ready to try the leap.

"Wait, Gem," Kathy looked worried. "I know you're good at leaps, but that's pretty hard."

Gemma stood on the end of the low beam and bounced on her toes.

"I know. That's the whole point," Gemma said. "If I can do better on the beam, then I won't have to be the worst at everything."

"Worst at everything?" Kathy shook her head. "You're not the worst at everything!" She still looked worried.

"You don't know what it's like . . . getting yelled at, having to do extra strength work!" Gemma's voice sounded loud. She felt angry at Michael, but somehow it sounded like she was angry at Kathy.

"He yells at me, too." Kathy looked hurt. Her face went pink. "He yells at all of us."

The two girls looked at each other.

Gemma still felt angry, but she didn't want to fight with Kathy.

"Who yells at you?" Suddenly, Michael was standing next to the low beam. He had his hands on his hips.

He was frowning more than ever.

Gemma jumped off the low beam. But it was too late—she had been caught.

Kathy's face had stopped looking pink. Now it was bright red.

"Have you been on this beam, Kathy?" Michael said.

Kathy shook her head. She looked like she wanted to cry.

"Then you can go home now," Michael said.

Kathy picked up her bag and looked at Gemma before she walked away. It was just a quick glance, but it was enough. *Good luck*, it said.

Michael turned to Gemma.

"What do you think you're doing?" Michael yelled. The whole gym went quiet. "Have you thought about what might happen if you hurt yourself here? With no coach? What on earth were you thinking?"

Gemma looked at Michael, but she didn't want to say she was sorry. She was sick of being yelled at.

"Well?" Michael said.

Gemma swallowed the lump in her throat. She couldn't cry. Not now.

"Sorry!" she yelled through a sob. But

she didn't want to say she was sorry. That didn't come out right at all.

Michael put his head to the side.

"Gemma, calm down," he said.

Calm down! Michael always yelled—that wasn't calm. Now Gemma couldn't stay calm either. "My parents pay you tons of money, and all you do is yell at me!" Gemma was surprised—she wasn't planning to say that, either. It just came out that way.

All you do is yell at me!

Michael looked even more surprised. "Come up to my office, Gemma," he said.

Gemma stomped up to Michael's office. But she didn't sit down. She still felt angry and annoyed.

"Sit down, Gemma," said Michael. He sounded worried. "You can talk to me."

"Talk to you?" Gemma said quietly.

She still didn't sit down.

Then, suddenly, it all came out.

"I did talk to you. I said I was sorry!" Gemma yelled. "I said I was sorry I kicked you. I'm SORRY!"

Michael looked at Gemma with his mouth open.

Gemma puffed hard. "But it was an

accident," she said. "I didn't do it on purpose. I didn't mean to kick you and I said I was sorry."

A tear slid down her cheek and she wiped it away.

Gemma kept going. "But you gave me the extra strength work and you yell at me all the time. It's not fair. I didn't do it to you on purpose, but you keep yelling at me."

That was it. It was out.

Gemma sat down.

Now, it was Michael's turn to stand up. He walked over to the window, rubbing his chin.

"I didn't realize you were so upset,"

Michael said quietly, looking out the window. "Sometimes I forget how young you girls are."

Michael looked out the window for a long time. So long that Gemma started to feel worried. What was Michael thinking? At least when he yelled, you could tell what he was thinking.

Now, Gemma had no idea what to expect.

CHAPTER EIGHT

Gemma sat in Michael's office feeling worried. How did she get herself into this mess? She had just yelled at an adult—her coach! What happens to a gymnast who yells at her coach?

But Gemma had no reason to worry.

When Michael sat down, his face looked kind and a bit sad. Even his bushy eyebrows didn't seem so gruff. When he spoke, his voice sounded calm. He even said he was sorry for yelling. It almost felt like he was talking to a friend, or maybe his daughter. He spoke slowly and explained a lot.

It turned out that the extra strength was not punishment. It was to help Gemma get strong—strong enough to do good handsprings. And it had worked. Michael said that Gemma's vaults were getting better and better.

As Michael talked, Gemma started feeling a bit happier. It didn't sound like he hated her after all. Michael said that he yelled at Gemma simply because it worked. Each time he yelled, she jumped a bit higher and ran a bit harder.

"I don't yell because I'm angry, Gemma," Michael said. "I yell to help you get better."

Gemma nodded. She started to feel a bit silly about getting so upset.

"When I yell at Fiona, she just gets scared," Michael said. "Naomi hardly listens when I yell. But you, Gemma, you listen and improve."

Michael paused. "I wouldn't normally say this," he said, "but you have the right mix of skill and guts, Gemma."

Gemma gulped. Michael was talking as though she wasn't the worst gymnast. He was talking as though she could be really good!

"I suppose I yell at you because I know

how good you could be," Michael said.

Gemma gulped again. Suddenly, she didn't feel sad or angry anymore. She felt fantastic. All that yelling was a good thing. And all that work—the sore muscles, the extra effort—she was really getting better.

Gemma felt so good that she couldn't stay quiet. Right away she told Michael about her plan for the beam.

"So that's what you were doing. . . ." Michael said. His voice sounded normal—gruff—again. But Gemma didn't mind.

"Let's make a deal," Michael said. "If you only work on the leap during class, I'll help you with it. It's not safe on your own."

Gemma grinned.

Michael thinks I could be good?

This was fantastic.

"But I want to see your beam routine finished by next Friday," Michael said. "After then, it's too close to the state finals to change your routine."

Gemma's mouth dropped open.

Next Friday?

That was only a week and a half away.

Then there was a knock at the door.

It was Gemma's dad. "I'm looking for

Gemma," he said, as he opened the door. He looked at Gemma. "Is everything alright?" he asked.

Both men looked at Gemma.

"Yes, uh, sorry," Gemma jumped up. She had made her dad wait in the car while she yelled at her coach. It was all turning out even more weird than when Gemma had given Michael a bloody nose.

On the way home, Gemma told her dad everything. It all came out at once. Suddenly, she didn't feel like she had to hide it. Doing the bad vault, feeling like the worst gymnast—she didn't have to hold it all inside.

When Gemma talked about kicking Michael, her dad chuckled.

"Wish I'd seen that one," her dad said.

For the rest of the evening, Gemma thought about her beam routine. How could she manage to do the switch leap in a week and a half? Even with Michael helping her, Gemma didn't know if she could do it by then.

But now, Gemma wanted to do the new leap more than ever. Michael thought she could be a good gymnast. Gemma wanted to be the best she could be. If she worked hard, she knew she could do it.

Gemma had a lot of work to do before the state finals, and there wasn't much time.

CHAPTER NINE

The next gym class started with a team meeting. The girls sat on the floor while Michael stood over them with his hands on his hips.

In many ways, nothing had changed. Michael still frowned and yelled. Fiona still looked scared. Naomi prodded a blister on her hand and didn't seem to listen.

But for Gemma, everything had changed.

When Michael yelled, she didn't feel scared or angry anymore. She felt like a real gymnast with a big competition ahead. The state finals were important. They were important enough to yell about.

After the talk, the team started on the beam. Michael took Gemma aside.

"Go, Gem," Kathy whispered. Then she walked to the high beam.

Gemma had called Kathy after the last gym class. The girls had giggled and chatted for an hour about the talk in Michael's office.

Gemma called out, "Thanks, Kathy." She was excited and a bit scared about doing her switch leap on the beam.

She showed Michael a switch leap on the floor near the low beam. She did a good leap, but still wobbled.

Michael shook his head. "You're leaping like you do on floor," he said gruffly. "You don't have to leap so high. Just keep your shoulders straight." Then he walked away.

Gemma tried again. She kept her shoulders straight—*run, run, switch leap, land*.

She didn't leap so high, but she landed a bit better. How strange. She had been trying to leap higher, but that had been the wrong thing to do.

Gemma smiled to herself. He was loud. He was gruff. But Michael was a really good coach.

Gemma kept practicing the leap during gymnastics until Michael called her to work on her other routines. At home, Gemma practiced wherever she could.

For the whole week and a half, Gemma worked on the leap. If she wasn't eating, sleeping, or at school, she was practicing the leap.

Finally, just in time for the Friday class, Gemma could land the switch leap on the low beam. She felt solid and safe.

But Michael still wouldn't let her do it on the high beam.

"Please, Michael," Gemma asked as the team walked to the high beam. "I know I can do it." If she didn't do the leap on the high beam today, she couldn't do it in the state finals.

Michael looked at Gemma.

"It's close. . . ." Michael said quietly.

"Come on, Michael," Naomi said. The whole team knew about Gemma's new leap. "It's only a leap."

"It's a very dangerous leap," Michael said, frowning. "But OK. Let's see it on the high beam, Gemma."

Gemma climbed up and stood at the end of the high beam. It always felt a lot higher when she was up there. She could feel the narrow bar of wood under her feet and her heart pumping in her chest. If she didn't land this, she could really hurt herself.

She wiped her hands on her legs.

Run, run . . . shoulders straight . . . switch leap . . . land.

That was it. Gemma landed squarely on the high beam. She didn't even wobble a bit.

The other girls clapped and smiled. Michael nodded his head. Gemma jumped off the high beam, grinning.

This was brilliant. Gemma used to be the worst gymnast. But not anymore. Now she was going to do a switch leap on the beam for the state finals!

All that extra work was worth it!

CHAPTER TEN

It was the day of the state finals. Everyone looked nervous. Kathy kept frowning and jumping on the spot. Anika and Fiona stayed stretching on the floor as though they were trying to hide. Even Naomi seemed quieter than normal.

But to anyone who didn't know them, the team looked good. The girls looked fresh. They all had their hair tied back with ribbons in the team colors. They all wore the team tracksuits—purple with two white stripes down the side. They looked like a real gymnastics team, warming up for the state finals.

The state gym seemed huge. It was busy with other teams of level sixes. Some girls looked around nervously. Others giggled as they twirled around the bars or tumbled on the floor.

It was a very big day.

Through the color and movement, Gemma could just see her parents sitting up in the stands. They sat still. It didn't even look like they were talking. They seemed to be a long way away.

Inside, Gemma felt strange. She felt nervous and excited at the same time. Today she had to do a switch leap on the beam in front of judges! Would she be able to do it?

To make things worse, the team was last on the beam. And Gemma was the last gymnast on her team. That meant Gemma would be nervous about her big leap right to the end.

Then Michael called a team meeting.

"OK, level six," Michael said. He was frowning, but Gemma thought she could see a sparkle in his eyes behind the bushy eyebrows. "You've done these routines hundreds of times. You all know what to do."

Michael paused. The five girls stood quietly at the start of the runway. The noise and movement seemed to disappear.

"I know you can do it," Michael said kindly. "Make me proud, level six."

The team stayed quiet, but the girls seemed to relax a bit. Kathy stopped frowning. Fiona almost looked like she could smile again. Michael's talk had helped them all.

All the nerves and excitement and fear settled. Now Gemma felt calm inside. She had worked hard and she knew what to do.

Now it was time to do it.

When it was Gemma's turn on the vault, she felt ready. She felt strong all over. She

OK....
Here I go!

wiped her hands on her legs, and waited. Then one of the judges nodded her head.

Gemma ran. Her legs pounded up the runway. All she could see was the vault ahead of her.

Run, run, legs together, butt tucked in....

As she sprang over the vault, her body lifted. For a second, it felt like she was flying. Then Gemma felt the ground beneath her.

She landed well.

It was a good vault.

When her score came up, Gemma felt even better. Gemma's score was the second highest in the team, just under Naomi's.

Kathy gave Gemma a big pat on the back.

Gemma sighed. This was great.

She didn't have to worry about being the worst gymnast anymore.

She did well on the bars and floor, too. She swung between the bars as though she had done it all her life. She tumbled high and danced with grace on floor. After all the hard work, today almost felt easy.

When it was time for the beam, Gemma waited quietly while the other four girls had their turns.

Finally, it was Gemma's turn on the beam. Some of the other teams had finished and sat quietly, watching.

It felt as though everyone in the gym was watching.

As Gemma started her routine, she thought of the gymnast on the Olympics video. She had done her routine in front of the whole world! Gemma knew she could do her routine in front of the state gym.

It felt great being up on the beam. When it was time for the switch leap, Gemma did it beautifully. No problem. She landed solidly and safely.

Behind her, she heard a gasp from another team coach.

When Gemma's score came up, everyone in the state gym clapped. It was a very high score.

Gemma felt proud, but she was also in a daze. She didn't understand what her high score really meant.

Michael kept smiling and saying, "Well done, Gemma."

Kathy and Anika took turns hugging Gemma. Then they hugged each other.

At one point, Naomi said quietly, "What did I do wrong?"

It wasn't until the presentation that Gemma understood what was happening. When it was time to award the highest score, they called Gemma's name.

Gemma had the highest overall score for level sixes in the state!

She stood on a platform and a judge gave her a trophy. Gemma couldn't stop grinning. Her whole team clapped. Even Naomi was smiling.

Gemma looked for her parents in the crowd. But they weren't in their seats. They had come down to the railing and were leaning over, clapping. Gemma's mom was smiling and crying all at once. Her dad kept punching the air with joy.

Standing on the platform, watching it all, was the best feeling.

It wasn't until going home in the car that Gemma finally had a chance to take a good look at her trophy. She turned it over in her hand and touched the cool gold. It glinted in the evening light.

The trophy showed a gymnast in a perfect handstand. She was upside down, with her legs straight and her toes pointed. But to Gemma, the trophy showed more than that.

Gemma ran her finger along the gymnast's straight legs.

To Gemma, the gymnast on the trophy was on her way over the vault in a handspring. Her butt was tucked in. Her legs were tight together. She was just about to push off the vault and lift up into the air to land.

The trophy was the best thing Gemma had ever been given. It showed everything Gemma had worked for.

To Gemma, the trophy showed a gymnast doing the best handspring ever.

✽THE END✽

GO GIRL!

If you loved reading about Gemma, you should meet the other **GO GIRL!** girls.

GO GIRL!

LUNCHTIME RULES
BY VICKI STEGGALL

❋ **Ant**

GO GIRL!

THE SECRET CLUB
BY CHRISSIE PERRY

★ **Tasmin**

GO GIRL!

SISTER SPIRIT
BY THALIA KALKIPSAKIS

✄ **Cassie**

Go Girl! #3

SISTER SPIRIT

BY
THALIA KALKIPSAKIS

My big sister Hannah hates me and I know why. It's because I was born after her.

When Hannah was three, I was born. Everyone said I was *sooooooo cute!* Mom says they stopped saying Hannah was cute, so she threw all my baby clothes down the toilet.

I look younger than I really am. I'm nine years old, but sometimes people think I look six or seven.

Hannah calls me a baby doll, but she doesn't mean it in a nice way. She says I should try to look my age, but it's not my fault! I can't change how I look.

But now, it's even worse than ever. Hannah cut off my hair and Mom went crazy on her. Then Hannah stopped talking to me.

Strange, isn't it? Hannah cut off my hair and got into trouble, and she blames me for it!

She must really hate me, that girl. Let me explain.

We were watching TV and a show came on about hair. It said that a haircut can change the way you look. It can make you look older or younger.

Hannah said, "Maybe if we cut your hair, people wouldn't think you're so cute anymore!"

"Yeah," I said, not really listening.

Hannah turned off the TV. "Aren't you sick of people saying how cute you look?" she asked.

"Yeah," I said again, but now I *was* listening.

"So why don't we cut your hair short, so you look your age?" Hannah said.

I wasn't sure. It sounded exciting, cutting my hair. I liked the idea of doing something different and looking older. But it's a big thing to cut off all your hair. And I've had long hair all my life.

"But what would Mom say?" I said.

"Mom!" Hannah rolled her eyes. Her hair is dark and shoulder length. It kinks up around her ears.

"Why do you always worry what Mom thinks? It's not Mom's hair, " she said.

She had a point. It wasn't Mom's hair, it was *my* hair.

"Come on, let's do it." Hannah's eyes looked bright with excitement.

It was exciting to do something like this together, just her and me. It felt a little like the stories you read of sisters going shopping and trying on clothes together. It felt good—like Hannah liked me.

It also seemed a bit naughty to do something without Mom knowing.

"OK," I said. "Let's do it."

Hannah smiled.

I bet my eyes looked as bright and excited as Hannah's.